Gift of Gab
and
Family Face-Off

POCKET
BOOKS

Pocket Books/Nickelodeon

London New York Sydney

Based on the TV series *The Wild Thornberrys* created by Klasky Csupo, Inc. as seen on *Nickelodeon*

POCKET
BOOKS

First published in Great Britain in 2003 by Pocket Books.
An imprint of Simon & Schuster UK Ltd
Africa House, 64–78 Kingsway, London WC2B 6AH

Originally published in the USA as separate volumes *Gift of Gab* and *Family Face-Off* in 2000 by Simon Spotlight, an imprint of Simon & Schuster Children's Division, New York

A CIP catalogue record for this book is available from the British Library

ISBN 0743469100

Printed and bound in the UK
1 3 5 7 9 10 8 6 4 2

Gift of Gab

adapted by Cathy East Dubowski
and Mark Dubowski
from the teleplay by Eva Almos
and Ed Scharlach
illustrated by the Thompson Bros.

Prologue

Hi! I'm Eliza Thornberry. I'm twelve years old and part of your average family. I have a dad, a mum, and a teenage sister named Debbie. Well, there *is* Donnie – we found him in the jungle. And Darwin the chimpanzee? He found us.

Oh, yeah, about our house. It moves! It's a big safari-van called a Commvee. It's got a table and places to sleep and just about everything we need to camp

1

anywhere. Would you believe it travels on land and water? We really need it because we travel all over the world. You see, my dad hosts this TV nature show and my mum films it.

Okay, so maybe we're not that average. And between you and me, something amazing happened to me. It's really cool, but totally secret. And you know what? Life's never been the same . . .

Do you want to know my secret? Well . . . promise not to tell anyone? Okay.

The secret is . . . I can talk to animals!

Here's the story of how it all began . . .

Chapter 1

I'm the luckiest girl in the world!

That's what I thought as my family drove through the hot, dusty streets of a small village in western Nigeria.

Our first adventure – Africa! It was so different from home. But that's what I liked about it.

Mum and Dad had travelled here to make their very first nature film. It was so cool that Debbie and I got to come along.

But Debbie didn't think so. She wasn't even looking out the window. She was too busy polluting the air by painting her toenails with smelly red nail polish.

Suddenly Dad shouted, "Everyone have a look-see up that tree!" He was so excited, he totally forgot to watch his driving. The Commvee swerved back and forth. "It's a rare white-throated bee-eater! Somebody pinch me!"

Mum pinched him.

"Ouch!" Dad yelped, then added, "Thanks, pumpkin. And look," he gushed, "we've caught it actually eating a bee!"

Dad jerked the wheel. Debbie and I tumbled to the floor.

"Nigel, dear," Mum said, "maybe you'd enjoy the sights a little more if *I* were driving – and you *weren't*."

"Smashing idea, Marianne!" Dad said. He let go of the steering wheel and leaned out the window for a better look.

Unfortunately, he was still in the driver's seat.

Mum didn't freak out. She simply grabbed the wheel and steered our huge Commvee safely down the road.

I never did see that white-throated bee-eater. But that was okay. I had a feeling we'd see lots of unusual wildlife soon.

An hour or so later Mum stopped the Commvee in the middle of a clearing. It was the perfect place to make camp.

I looked out of the window. Wow! This is so cool! Debbie was mad because she wanted to stay in a fancy hotel. But not me. Hotels are boring! With our Commvee we could sleep right out here in the middle of the wilderness. Who knew what we'd see?

I flew out of the Commvee. I was happy to be out in the fresh air – and away from

Debbie's stinky nail polish!

Mum and Dad quickly unpacked and set up their equipment – cameras, tripods, light meters, microphones – they were ready to film the beginning of their documentary.

"Hello," Dad said into the camera in his cheery British accent. (Dad is from England.) "Welcome to *Nigel Thornberry's Animal World* . . ."

They would be busy for a while. That was okay with me. I was ready to explore the world!

When I was younger, Debbie used to play with me. But now she acts too cool to play. I mean, there we were, surrounded by the African jungle, full of untold secrets. And what did she do?

She sat down at the picnic table and dumped out all her makeup. Then she stared into a mirror at a pimple on the end of her nose that nobody else could even see.

Who cared? I set out to explore by myself.

The jungle around our clearing was thick and green. Suddenly I saw a cute, little grey chimpanzee standing a few yards away.

I didn't move. I didn't want to frighten it. "Hi, there," I said softly. I hoped I sounded friendly.

The chimpanzee shrieked and ducked back into the bushes.

Oh, if only I could talk to it. Really talk to it – in its own language. Then I could tell it not to be afraid. Hey! Maybe I can pretend to talk Chimpanzee! I leaned down and quietly chattered like a chimp.

The chimp stared back like it couldn't tell what to make of me. Then it scratched its head – and chattered back!

I felt like jumping up and down and cheering! But I didn't want to scare it. So I yanked on my pigtails and made more chimp-like sounds. I had no idea what I was saying. I hoped I hadn't accidentally said anything rude!

At last the chimp smiled. Slowly it came out of the bushes. Then it walked right up to me! Cool! No wonder my dad had picked studying nature for a career.

I saw that my parents were taking a break. So I led the chimp over to show my family. "Look what I found!"

My parents looked up in surprise.

"Fascinating!" Dad exclaimed. "They're not usually such social creatures."

Debbie's mirror flashed in the sunlight. The chimp wandered over towards the picnic table to see.

Debbie had her hair pulled back in a ponytail. She was putting some kind of weird goop on her face and neck.

The curious chimp looked over her shoulder into the mirror.

"Ewww!" Debbie screamed. She jumped up and threw a jar of face cream at it. "Get away from me, you chimpan-geek!"

The chimp cried and ran back into the bushes.

I was so mad! My parents love animals. And so do I. What was Debbie's problem?

"Debbie!" I exclaimed. "It didn't do anything! You don't treat a little animal like that!"

Debbie glared at me. "It seems to work with you!"

It was a mean thing to say. But I didn't care. I was too worried about the chimp. I turned and ran after it.

"Eliza! Wait!" Mum called after me.

But I had already disappeared into the jungle.

Chapter 2

"Hello!" I called out as I wandered deeper into the jungle. "Here, little chimp!" There were so many places here for an animal to hide. How could I ever find it?

I climbed over a log and kept walking. The trees and bushes seemed to move. I heard strange squawks and cheeps and growls. Were they friendly sounds? I wished I could understand what they meant.

Suddenly I heard a weird snorting noise – kind of like a pig eating peanut butter and jelly.

There, in the distance, lay a fat brown animal. It seemed to be rolling in the dirt.

As I crept closer, I heard a strange sound. A horrible sound. A sound like . . . pain!

I ran towards the animal. It was a large, hairy, warty warthog. I was surprised that it didn't run away.

And then I saw why.

The warthog's left hind leg was caught in the jaws of a big steel trap.

"Oh, you poor piggy!" I gasped. I can't stand to see animals in pain. I reached out to pet it. But it growled and lashed out at me with two big tusks that stuck out on either side of its mouth.

"I won't hurt you," I said in a soft voice. "I've got to get you out of there!"

I stood where I could reach its hind leg

— but where its scary teeth couldn't reach me! I tried to pull the trap open.

"Uhn!" I grunted as I struggled.

At first it wouldn't budge. The trap held the warthog's leg tight between its jagged teeth.

But I wouldn't give up. I *love* animals. Which means I also *hate* traps.

I tried again. My arms trembled as I pulled the steel jaws apart a few inches. But it was enough. The warthog pulled its leg free!

Then I let go.

Clang!

The force of the trap snapping shut sent me flying head over heels to the ground.

The fierce-looking warthog snorted and got to its feet. It trotted over and stared down at me.

I had freed the animal from the trap. But now *I* was trapped!

"Looks like your leg's okay now," I said with a shaky smile.

The beast took a step towards me. I gasped as it growled and shook its tail.

Then something amazing happened. It was one of the strangest things I have ever seen! A grass skirt appeared around the warthog's thick waist. A front hoof twisted, then morphed into – a human hand! And then it had two hands!

The warthog's groans were frightening, but I couldn't run. I couldn't stop watching.

Its back legs turned into – human legs! And then its big, hairy, warty face morphed into – a big, hairy, warty *human* face!

I closed my eyes and shook my head. Then I opened my eyes again. "No way!" I cried.

The fat, warty warthog had changed into . . . a fat, warty man!

Chapter 3

I rubbed my eyes. Was I seeing things?

I opened my eyes again. The man was still there.

He wore a feathered headdress and a grass skirt. His face looked a lot like the warthog's – same eyes, brown hair, plenty of warts, big belly. He even had a big bone through his nose.

The man seemed as surprised as I was. He wiggled his fat fingers. Then he threw his hands in the air and laughed. "I'm human again!" he shouted. "After all these years!" He shook my hand hard. "Oh, thank you, little girl!"

I stared at him. "But I saved a warthog!" I said. "How did you become a man?"

The man shrugged. "I guess you broke the spell."

I heard a huge rumbling sound. The man grabbed his belly. "Ooh. Got anything to eat? I'm starved."

I pulled an apple from my pocket. The man grabbed it and gobbled it down. Maybe he had changed into a man. But he still had the manners of a warthog!

Especially when he let out a big, deep "B-u-u-u-r-r-r-r-p!"

"Nice burp!" I said. Then I frowned. "What spell?"

The man began to snack on the leaves of a bush. "I used to be a high shaman in the Sarimba tribe," he explained. "We were a people who believed that animal and human spirits joined together. But the truth was, I couldn't stand animals!"

"That's terrible!" I said.

"That's what the Sarimbas said! Then I ate the really high shaman's prized sheep. He was so angry, he cast a spell that turned me into a warthog. But thanks to you, I've turned back into a man!"

"Because I saved your life?" I asked.

"Exactly." The shaman leaned closer. "The spell could only be broken if a human really cared about me. But they figured, who would like a gross, smelly animal?"

"I would," I said.

"That's why I get to grant you a wish!" the shaman exclaimed.

"I get a wish?" I gasped. "Wow!" I couldn't believe it! The shaman waited patiently while I thought and thought.

Wouldn't you know it? My mind was a total blank! Then I heard a familiar sound. I looked into the trees. It was the little grey chimpanzee! "Hey!" I called.

The chimp chattered and hid among the leaves.

"I'm not going to hurt you!" I promised. But the chimp wouldn't come out. I sighed. "Oh, don't you understand?"

My heart sank. The little chimp was so cute. I *really* wanted to be friends with it. If only I could talk to it!

And then I smiled. I knew exactly what I wanted to wish for! "I want to be able to talk to animals!" I told the shaman.

"Well, that's a first," the shaman replied. "Let's see now, how does that one go . . ." Sparkles swirled around the shaman's right hand. And then –

Poof!

A stick with the head of a snake on one

end appeared in his hand. It was some kind of magic wand. The shaman raised his magic stick to the heavens and shouted, "OOBALA-BOOBALA BOOBALA-DOOBALA! Give this one a shadoo-bah!"

I held my breath. Nothing happened.

The shaman said, at last, scratching his head, "Hmm. Wrong one. How about – OOOBALABOOBALABOOBALA! She can talk to animals!"

This time *something* happened. A strange whirl of blue light spun from the mouth of the snake head on the end of the magic stick. It swirled around me. It nearly took my breath away. I watched as ancient symbols of animals danced in the swirling light. I could hear their squawks and growls and roars.

I was terrified. The shaman's magic was real! I felt so dizzy. With a gasp, I tumbled to the ground.

Chapter 4

I waited for the world to stop spinning. I caught my breath and blinked. I looked around. All signs of the magic were gone. The clearing was quiet and peaceful again.

"It's time for me to go!" the shaman said.

But what about my wish? I didn't feel any different. Had the magic worked? Did it come with instructions? "Hey, wait!" I cried.

But the shaman had disappeared.

Was this a joke? Was it a dream?

"Hey, that's my gerbil!" someone shouted.

"Gulp! Not anymore!" somebody replied.

I looked up into a nearby tree. Two meerkats were arguing. And I understood *every* word they said! The shaman's magic had worked! "Wow!" I exclaimed. "I understood that!"

I wandered farther into the jungle. "Hello," I called out. "Can anybody understand me?"

"There's a bug in your hair!" someone sang out in a cheerful British accent. "Can I have it?"

"Eeew!" I brushed at my hair. Then I realised: somebody answered me! I looked up. It was the chimp I'd met that morning! "Wow!" I said. "You said that, didn't you?"

He sat up with a startled look on his face. "Wait a minute! *You're* speaking *Chimp*!"

"Yes!" I cried. "And I can't even speak French!"

The chimp dropped to the ground.

"Finally!" he exclaimed gleefully. "Someone *civilised* to talk to!"

"Finally!" I exclaimed just as gleefully. "Someone *uncivilised* to talk to!"

We grabbed each other's hands and laughed. I just knew we were going to be friends.

Chapter 5

The chimp showed me how to swing through the trees on vines. I told him all about my family. Hanging from both hands, I said, "By the way, I'm Eliza."

"My name is AH-ooh-ooh-ah," he screeched. "But my friends call me AH!"

"That's a little hard for me to say," I said. "Why don't I just call you . . ." I thought a moment. "Darwin?"

"I like that," the chimp said.

I smiled. "We have so much to talk about. Maybe you can stay with us!"

"Really?" Darwin exclaimed. "I thought you'd never ask!" Then he frowned. "But your parents might not want me to."

"Sure, they will," I insisted. "I'll talk them into it." I grabbed Darwin's hand and led him back to my family's camp. Darwin scampered over to our clothesline. He seemed spellbound by the freshly washed clothes.

"Hey," I said, "do you want to dress like us, too?"

Darwin nodded, so I pulled some clothes off the line. He smiled in delight as I slipped a blue-and-white-striped tank top over his head. Next I gave him a pair of blue shorts. I held up a mirror for him to see.

Darwin smiled. I could tell he was happy.

Then I heard my parents and sister coming out of the jungle. I hoped they were in a good mood. I wanted to ask if I could have a friend to sleep over. Would they mind that my new friend was a chimp?

Mum and Dad were smiling. But Debbie stomped into camp as if she'd had the worst day of her life. She didn't even see Darwin at first. She dropped some equipment on the ground at his feet.

Then Debbie saw Darwin. "Ewwwwww!" she shrieked. Her eyes grew wide as she stared at Darwin's clothes. "Wait! I am going to barf! Is that revolting hair ball wearing my lucky top? Give it back!" she shouted. But when she saw him scratch, she turned away in disgust. "Eww! Just keep it!"

Darwin ran to my side. He was trembling. But when I took him by the hand, he seemed to calm down.

"Mum! Dad!" I said. "Guess what! I can talk to animals!"

My parents stared at me in astonishment.

I giggled. "I know it sounds crazy, but I really can."

At least, that was what I *tried* to say.

But something was wrong. Super wrong!

I suddenly realised why my parents were staring at me.

My thoughts didn't come out in human words. The sounds coming from my mouth were *animal* sounds!

"Eliza, is this a joke, honey?" my mother asked. "Why are you croaking like a frog?"

"I told you she was a loon," Debbie complained.

I shivered. I didn't know *what* was going on. I cleared my throat and tried again. "Mum, Dad, I can talk to animals . . ."

This time, all my words sounded like gorilla!

Dad grinned in delight. He thought I was playing a game.

But this was no game. It was totally for real!

I tried to speak to them again. But all I could do was growl, chirp, cheep, hoot, and bark.

I turned to my new friend. "Oh, no, Darwin! Is this really happening? The shaman's spell – he got it all wrong!" I looked at my family – the people I loved more than anything in the world.

"I can talk to animals," I said. "But now I can't talk to *people*!"

Chapter 6

There was only one thing to do.

"Come on, Darwin," I cried. "We've got to find that shaman!"

Of course, to my family, it sounded like I said, "Oooh-ooh, eek-eek, squawk!"

I ran into the jungle with Darwin right behind me.

"Be back by nightfall, honey," my mum called after me. "Remember, we're leaving for Kenya!"

One thing about the jungle that's different from towns: There are no street signs. So if you want to find your way, you have to know how to read other signs. Like take a left at the tangled vine. Then look for three big rocks covered with slime.

I tried to remember which vines, rocks, bushes, and trees I'd seen on my way to the place where I met the shaman. But I kept getting mixed up.

At last Darwin and I came to a clearing in the jungle. Was this the spot? It was hard to be sure.

But one thing *was* for sure.

"He's not here," I said. "He's probably gone forever."

"Darwin, what am I going to do?" I exclaimed. I sat down on a big rock and propped my head in my hands. "I can't talk to my family anymore. What if I'm like this for the rest of my life?"

"Don't worry, Eliza," Darwin said. "You can still talk to *me*."

"I wanted to talk to animals so badly . . . ," I began. My throat clogged up. Tears began to trickle down my face.

Darwin sat down beside me. Tears welled up in his eyes, too. "Don't cry," he said with a sniffle. "You'll get me started and my nose will get all runny and my fur will get all matty and . . ." Darwin burst into tears and threw his arms around me.

Suddenly I heard a rumbling sound. The sound grew louder and louder. A huge shadow blocked out the setting sun.

I wiped my nose and looked up.

A tour bus drove by. It was old, red, and rickety. Many people sat inside.

Including a big, fat, warty-looking guy eating a chicken leg!

I jumped to my feet as the bus chugged

on by. "Darwin! It's the shaman guy! Come back! I need to talk to you!"

I tried to run after him, but it was no use. The bus was faster than I could ever run.

I watched as my one chance to get my wish fixed disappeared in a cloud of dust.

Chapter 7

Then I remembered my dad – the brilliant naturalist Nigel Thornberry. He was always wandering off to study some animal, bird, or bug. So he got lost a lot. Somehow though, he always managed to find his way back home. You know what he always says?

"Heads up! Carry on! Never say die. Come on, Eliza. You'll never get anywhere by sitting on your duff, my dear! A journey of a

thousand miles begins with a single step . . ."

Well, my red hair isn't the only thing I got from my father. "Come on, Darwin. I'm going to find us a shortcut through the jungle so we can cut off that bus!"

We walked and walked. But there was no sign of the road.

"Where are we, Eliza?" Darwin asked. He sounded scared.

"I don't know." I sighed. "I wish there was someone I could ask. But then, I'd probably just bark at them."

Then it hit me. "But I *can* talk to animals!" I exclaimed. "*They'll* help us!"

"Or eat us . . . ," Darwin said.

"No, Darwin," I promised. "They're going to love me." I pulled him along the path. "You'll see."

I spotted some bearded monkeys in a tree. Darwin and I climbed up to ask directions.

Their answer was to tickle Darwin till he shrieked.

"Will you please tell us how to get to the road?" I asked.

But they just started tickling me! We had to get away.

I grabbed hold of a thick vine. Together we swung to another tree. We sat there dangling our feet as we caught our breath.

Suddenly I froze as a huge, ugly bird landed right next to me. A vulture! It was bigger than I was. It stared at me with big, scary eyeballs. And it looked awfully hungry . . .

"Uh, hello, nice vulture," I said politely.

I knew from Dad that vultures eat dead animals to help keep the Earth clean. This one looked at me like I was a cheeseburger. "Hmph! You're *way* too fresh for me to eat."

I gulped. "Um, sorry to bother you," I said politely. "But we got chased up this tree and we've got to find the –"

"Yeah, yeah, yeah," the vulture said rudely. Suddenly she pointed with her beak. "Hey! Look over there!"

Darwin and I looked.

The vulture spread her wings wide – and shoved the two of us right off the limb!

Darwin and I screamed. "Ahhhhhhh!"

Thud! Thud!

We landed in the dirt.

"What about now?" the vulture asked eagerly. "Are you starting to *fester* yet?"

I stood up. "No!" I replied. "And you didn't need to do that!"

The vulture just spread her wings and flew away.

"So, I'm seeing that all animals aren't so friendly," I said.

"Depends on who you talk to."

I looked up. That wasn't Darwin's voice! Who said that?

A white horse-like animal with two twisted horns on his head trotted into the clearing. "Some of us are charming," he added.

"Are you some kind of antelope?" I asked.

"They're my cousins! I'm a hartebeest," the animal said proudly. "Are you some kind of talking girl?"

"Yup. I'm an Eliza Thornberry," I said. "Do you know what a 'road' is?"

"Sure," the hartebeest said.

"Do you think you could take us there?" I asked.

The hartebeest shrugged. "I'm free most of the day." He bent his front leg and made an elegant bow. "Hop on!"

I climbed on and pulled Darwin up behind me. Then the hartebeest headed straight for the road.

Or so I thought.

We rode for half an hour. Then the hartebeest said, "Now, I know *what* a road is. I just don't know *where* it is."

My heart sank. I felt Darwin's arms hug me tight.

"So we're *all* lost," I said.

Chapter 8

I felt like giving up.

But then I jerked my head up at the sound of squawking. A flock of beautiful red birds stared down at us. Yes! I had an idea!

I quickly told the birds my problem. From high in the sky it was easy for them to spot the road we needed. Looking up, it was easy for us to follow them. Within minutes we had found the road.

"Thanks a lot, guys!" I called. "Have a

great time migrating to Cairo!"

The road wound up a rocky mountainside. Near the top, I spotted the bus parked by a fence. "That's it!" I cried.

Darwin and I jumped down from the hartebeest's back. "Thanks for the ride!" I exclaimed. The animal bowed, then he gracefully sprang off into the jungle.

At the top of the cliff we found lots of people waiting in line. But I didn't see the shaman anywhere.

"Five naira," said a man who sat near the entrance. When the people paid, he handed them a towel. "Enjoy the mud," he said. I figured the shaman must have gone inside.

Oops! The man dropped a towel. When he bent over to pick it up, Darwin and I dashed through the gate.

Inside we saw fat people. Skinny people. All soaking in mud baths. But nobody who looked like a warthog.

"*B-u-u-u-u-r-r-r-p!*"

I whirled around. "I'd know that burp anywhere!" I shouted.

Darwin and I ran towards the sound. We found the shaman up to his waist in mud. And he was still chewing on a chicken leg.

"Why did you disappear?" I demanded.

"To return to my old tribal hot springs," the shaman explained. "Ah! Nothing like a good mud wallow." He laughed.

"Look, mister, you goofed," I said. "I can't talk to people anymore!"

The shaman shrugged. "And that's a problem?"

"But I need to talk to my family!" I cried.

The shaman sighed. "Look, I can make you talk to animals *or* people – but not both. Who do you want to talk to?"

"This isn't fair!" I cried. "I've made a

new friend named Darwin. We talk about *everything*. But" – I swallowed the lump in my throat – "I guess I can't go through life without talking to people . . ."

Poof! Sparkles surrounded the shaman's fist. His magic stick appeared in his hand. "Okay, back to the way you were – "

"Wait!" I cried. "Wait – I just need a minute." I had to say goodbye to Darwin first. He was playing in his own pool of mud.

Slowly I walked over to him. He smiled at me. How could I tell him?

"Darwin," I said softly. "This has probably been the best day of my entire life! But . . . I need to talk to my mum. And my dad. And my sister – well, not so much to her. But you and me, Darwin – " I took a deep breath, then said the words I did not want to say – in any language: "We're not going to be able to understand each other anymore."

The look on his face nearly broke my

heart. Choking back tears, I said sadly, "There's nothing I can do . . ." I forced my feet to carry me back to the shaman.

The shaman raised his fist in the air and shouted: "BAREEPLE-MEEPLE, SHE-CAN-TALK-TO-PEOPLE . . . Leeple."

He pointed his magic stick at me again. A bright light and sparkling colours blew around me. Only this time the sounds of animals screamed louder. This time the winds were even stronger. I felt as if I might be whisked away into the sky.

But the magic tornado simply tossed me into Darwin's pool of mud. "Agh!" I gasped.

"What's going on?" Darwin asked as he hovered around me like a mother hen. "What's he doing? What . . ."

Then his words changed into the wild chatter of a chimpanzee. A chatter I could no longer understand. I stared at him with tears in my eyes.

It was time to go home.

"Goodbye, mister," I said to the shaman.

I guess I should have felt lucky. After all, I had talked to animals – if only for a little while. That was more than other people ever had in a whole lifetime.

As I walked away I heard Darwin scolding the shaman in Chimpanzee. He jumped up and down like a little kid having a temper tantrum.

But the muddy ground was slippery. He lost his balance. I watched in horror as he fell and skidded through the mud on his stomach – towards the edge of the cliff!

"Oh, no! Darwin!" I cried.

I didn't stop to think of my own safety. I just ran – slipping and sliding in the mud – to save my friend.

But it was too late.

Darwin screamed – and disappeared over the edge of the cliff!

Chapter 9

I couldn't bear to look!

But then I heard chatter. Frightened *chimp* chatter! *Darwin?*

I dropped to my hands and knees. Carefully I crawled to the edge of the cliff. I took a deep breath, then made myself look.

Darwin clung to a branch. He was alive!

But below him raged a roaring river. If Darwin fell, I knew I'd never see him again.

"I'm coming to get you!" I cried. "Hang on!"

A branch stuck out at the edge of the cliff. Perfect! I grabbed on tight, then scooted on my stomach to the edge. Slowly, carefully, I lowered myself down towards Darwin.

At last I hung down straight. I could almost reach him – but not quite. I pointed my foot, stretching for an extra inch.

Darwin reached up one of his hands and grabbed one of mine with a tight grip. Yes!

But the branch was not strong enough to hold me *and* Darwin. It tore away from the cliff! I screamed as we fell towards the river.

But there was no splash! I opened my eyes. Somehow I had grabbed the branch that Darwin had dangled from.

Snap!

That's when the branch broke in two! I heard a piece splash in the water below.

My hands ached. How much longer could I hold on?

"Grab on, Eliza!" a deep voice suddenly boomed.

I looked up. The shaman! He leaned over the edge of the cliff and held out one of his hands.

I grabbed on tight, and the shaman yanked us back up to the top.

Darwin and I lay gasping on the muddy ground. We were okay!

"Thank you!" I told the shaman. "Thank you! You saved us!"

The shaman looked embarrassed. But he smiled when he saw Darwin and me hugging like we'd just won a million dollars.

"Come on, Darwin," I said at last. "Let's go home."

As we walked away, Darwin chattered excitedly. But, of course, I couldn't understand a single word. That was the only sad part.

"Wait a minute," the shaman called out to us.

Darwin and I turned around.

The shaman's eyes had filled with tears. "I shouldn't be doing this, but – what the heck. There's a spell I heard about. Not an easy one. But if you're willing to give it a try, I am."

"Will I be able to talk to Darwin – and to people, too?" I asked.

"Yes! But if I get it wrong . . ." The shaman shrugged. "You might grow an extra head."

Ewww! That was a big risk. Was it worth it?

I looked at Darwin. Darwin looked at me and smiled. And I knew what I wanted to do. Good friends like Darwin aren't easy to find – in the city *or* in the jungle. When you find one, you should do all you can to hold on.

I turned back to the shaman. "Let's give it a try!"

"Okay," the shaman shouted. "Give her the deluxe spell!"

A dazzling orange light spun around me. The winds blew. Images of animals roared around my head.

Then the winds died. I fell to the ground on top of Darwin.

"Watch it!" Darwin complained.

I sat up. "I – I'm sorry. I –" Then my mouth hung open. I grabbed Darwin by the shoulders. "We're talking!"

"Yay!" he cried. We held hands and danced around.

"I can talk to *everything* now!" I shouted to the sky. I had never felt so happy in all my life!

The shaman climbed back into his mud bath and began to chomp on another chicken leg.

"I don't know how to thank you," I told him. "You've changed my life forever!"

He waved me over. "Just remember one thing," he warned me, his voice a whisper. "You must *never* tell a soul about these powers. If you do . . . the gift will disappear."

Never tell? Not even my mum and dad? How could he expect me to keep such a secret?

The shaman continued to stare at me.

I smiled. "I understand."

Then I ran to grab hold of Darwin's hand.

It was time to go home.

Chapter 10

It was dark by the time Darwin and I found our way back to camp. I saw my mum and dad in the moonlight. They were carrying a huge trunk towards the Commvee. They were packing up.

Oh, yeah. Tomorrow we were leaving for Kenya.

"Mum! Dad!" I cried. "Guess what?"

My parents gasped. I guess I did look kind of funny with mud smeared all over me.

But they didn't yell. They waited for me to explain where I had been.

I grinned. I was so full of wonderful feelings – stories of all the magical things that had happened to me in the jungle.

But then I remembered the shaman's warning.

"You must never tell a soul . . ."

No way was I going to risk losing this special gift!

So all I said was, "I have a new friend!" I reached out for Darwin's hand and pulled him into the circle of my family.

Darwin smiled a shy smile.

My dad seemed delighted. Mum shook her head in wonder. Debbie covered her face with her hands and groaned in horrified disgust.

But I didn't care. I had a wonderful new friend.

And now that I could talk to animals? I had a feeling the adventures had just begun.

Discovery Facts

Hartebeest: The hartebeest is an endangered species now that the African plains have become more developed. It is still a strong survivor. In fact, unlike many of its cousins, the hartebeest does not need drinking water as long as there are grasses and roots for it to graze on.

Meerkat: The meerkat looks like it is always wearing sunglasses because of the dark skin around its eyes which helps it to see in the bright light of the African plain. It lives in families of five to thirty members, known as "mobs."

Vulture: The vulture is a wild African scavenger – it eats the remains of dead animals. After a lion kill, the sky will fill with vultures, circling like planes over an airport, waiting their turn.

Warthog: Some say the warthog is Africa's ugliest animal, but not according to other warthogs! Like the elephant, the warthog is often hunted for its tusks. However, it is not nearly as protected by hunting laws as the elephant is.

About the Authors

Cathy East Dubowski and **Mark Dubowski** started writing and illustrating children's books while they lived in a small apartment in New York City. Now they work in two old barns on Morgan Creek near Chapel Hill, North Carolina. They live with their daughters, Lauren and Megan, and their two golden retrievers, Macdougal and Morgan. They also wrote the novelisations of both Rugrats feature films, *The Rugrats Movie* and *Rugrats in Paris,* and the Rugrats chapter books, *Chuckie's Big Wish* and *It Takes Two!*

Family Face-off

by Maria Rosado
illustrated by Bob Ostrom

Chapter 1

Eliza couldn't believe what her father, Nigel, was saying.

"It's true, Marianne," Nigel said. "Darwin's ideas truly are brilliant!"

"Brilliant?" Eliza asked in amazement. She poked her head through the trapdoor in the roof of the Commvee. Nigel and Marianne were steering the multipurpose vehicle through the seas off Ecuador. "You can't really be talking about Darwin?"

"We certainly are, poppet!" Nigel gushed. "Smashing, isn't it? We're going to the Galápagos islands to trace the path of Charles Darwin! The very man who made evolution a household word!"

"Of course!" Eliza said. "THAT Darwin." For a minute, she had thought they were talking about the chimpanzee who lived with the Thornberrys.

Eliza laughed as she told Darwin, the chimp, what had happened. He was also on the roof, and had been scratching himself with his foot.

"They could've been talking about me," Darwin whined.

"Don't get me wrong, Darwin, I know you're brilliant," Eliza whispered to her best friend. "But they can't understand all the intelligent things you say."

"Humph," Darwin snorted.

Thanks to a mysterious shaman, Eliza

could understand Darwin — in fact, she could talk to just about any animal. And it was a secret!

On the horizon, a cluster of tiny lumps was getting larger. Soon they began to look more like islands — The Galápagos Islands. Its volcanic peaks were covered in a fog that drifted away just as the Commvee arrived at Santa Cruz Island.

The Thornberrys headed for the Charles Darwin Research Station to check in with a ranger.

Donnie ran ahead, waving and shouting, "SibeeDARwoowoo!"

Donnie was a half-wild little boy the Thornberrys had found in Borneo. It was hard to understand anything he said. At the station, he tried to climb on the ranger's head.

"Ah, yes, the Thornberrys," the ranger said, as he pried Donnie away. "So happy

to have you back on our islands."

Funny, Eliza thought, he didn't look happy.

"Just remember," the ranger added, "you *must* not bring in any foods or animals which might upset the delicate balance of nature here. No plants, no seeds, and NO pets."

The ranger looked at Darwin.

"Darwin isn't a pet," Eliza protested. "He's a highly valued member of our family."

Darwin picked that moment to scratch his underarm.

"Uh, yes. Well." The ranger sniffed. "How interesting that two famous families would be here at the same time to make the exact same trip."

Nigel's eyes popped open. "What? Who?"

"Leo Léon," said the ranger. "From the show, *Leo Léon, King of the Beasts*."

"Yes, Leo with the ego," Marianne snorted as the ranger walked off.

But Nigel was hopping with excitement. Leo Léon was one of his idols!

"Smashing!" Nigel said, rubbing his hands in glee. "I'd love a chat."

"Who's Leo Léon?" Eliza asked.

Behind them, someone laughed. Eliza whirled around. Then she gasped. She seemed to be looking at a mirror image of her family!

Chapter 2

Except for his yellow hair, Leo could pass as Nigel's twin.

"Silly leetle girl!" Leo sneered. "Only stupid people do not know Leo Léon."

His evil twin, Eliza thought.

Standing beside Leo was his wife, Natasha. She wore a fancy French *chapeau* – otherwise she looked exactly like Marianne. Damien, Leo's teenage son, had wavy blond hair that fell in front of one eye, just like Debbie. There was even someone as wild-looking as Donnie: a very hairy little man wolfing down a chocolate snack.

"That is Marcel, our assistant," Leo said. "And this is Edmond!"

Eliza gasped. A boy, wearing glasses and braces, looked just like her! But, unlike Eliza, he also wore a sneer on his face and a parrot on his shoulder.

"Say 'hi, dweeb-o,' Napoleon," the boy told his parrot.

Nigel began introducing his own family.

"*Oui*. Yes, I know. I have seen your leetle show," Leo said, yawning. "*Seagull Tornbunny's Animal Farm*."

"It's *Nigel Thornberry's Animal World*," Marianne said.

Leo simply shrugged. "Whatever you say. Now, *moi* says that the Léons are here, so the Tornbunnys must go."

Nigel's jaw dropped. He was sure he must have heard wrong. "Er, I say, there's room for both of us! In fact, you're welcome to join us aboard the Commvee. We could join forces, you know!"

Leo looked down his enormous nose at the Commvee. "Pooh! Your leetle car is no good for such a trip."

Then he pointed towards the dock. "*Voila* . . . the Cleopatra!"

Nigel's mustache drooped at the sight of the Léons' vehicle. The Cleopatra looked like the perfect ship for someone as grand as Leo Léon. Suddenly Nigel felt that he and the Commvee were a little shabby.

Damien spoke up. "We have a remote locator system that can spot the smallest bug on the islands. Plus we can put out live TV coverage of our trip twenty-four hours a day!"

"*Oui,* that is right!" Leo said. "We broadcast all over the world."

Nigel's spirits sank more. How could anyone compete with that?

Marianne was worried, too. "Nigel, we've visited the islands before. Maybe we should just leave it to the Léons this time."

Leo laughed. "I knew you would not be able to keep up. Here, it is the 'survival of the fittest,' as Charles Darwin said."

"He didn't say that," Eliza said. She'd been reading about the scientist. "That was some other guy."

Leo pretended not to hear. "The one who will do *anything* to survive is always the winner!"

Eliza didn't agree. Neither did Marianne. "Nigel, I've changed my mind!" she said. "We *are* going to make this trip. We'll prove our way is just as good as his, and . . . well . . . much nicer!"

The Léons looked bored.

"Not only that, we'll do it *faster*," Marianne boldly added.

Suddenly Leo perked up. A race! He listened as Marianne suggested some rules: Both families must visit the four islands Darwin had. They had to spot every one of the animals Darwin had seen and get the proof on film. The first one to return with proof of all the species wins.

"All the species that still exist, that is," Marianne finished.

Leo nodded eagerly. "The whole world will be watching."

Nigel gulped. But Marianne called out after Leo as he and his family walked away. "You're on! And may the best family win!"

Chapter 3

Eliza was about to follow her parents back towards the Commvee when she heard a loud *CRACK!*

It was Edmond, the boy with the parrot. He had just smashed a walnut shell under his heel.

"Caw-haw! Napoleon wants a walnut!" his parrot sang. It gobbled up the nut.

Eliza warned Edmond, "Be careful. You're not allowed to bring seeds to the

Galápagos," she said. "It might mess up the whole food chain. And you could be kicked off the islands!"

Edmond looked thoughtful. "Thanks for the info!" he said, before dropping the walnuts into his pocket and walking away.

A minute later, from out of nowhere, Napoleon swooped down on Eliza and she fell. Edmond helped her up and dusted the sand off her clothes.

"I'm soooooo sorry!" he said. "I don't know what got into Napoleon."

Edmond seemed so kind and helpful, but Eliza thought she heard him snicker as he rushed off to the Cleopatra.

Not long after, the high-tech ship set sail. The Thornberrys were still busy loading supplies onto the Commvee.

Another rule of the race was that both families had to carry all they needed, just as Darwin's ship, the *Beagle*, did. If they ran out of anything, they'd have to go back to Santa Cruz Island to stock up.

"Debbie, please check the water supply," Marianne said. "Eliza, see what that ranger wants."

The ranger was marching up to the Commvee. He wanted to see Eliza.

"Young lady, I received a report that you're carrying seeds onto the islands!" said the ranger angrily. "Will you please empty your pockets?"

Eliza reached into her pockets – and pulled out a handful of walnuts!

"These aren't mine!" she shouted.

Ignoring Eliza, the ranger told Nigel and Marianne that the caller had warned that more nuts were hidden on board the Commvee. He needed to search the whole vehicle.

Eliza was furious! She was sure

Edmond had something to do with this. Even worse, the ranger now wanted the Thornberrys out of the race!

"After all, you broke the rules," he told Eliza.

"But I didn't put them there!"

"Can you prove they came from someplace else?" asked the ranger.

Eliza stomped off while the ranger finished his search. She watched a hawk fly down near the Cleopatra.

"Hawww, hawww! Greedy parrot," Eliza heard the hawk grumble. "All he left is shells, shells, shells!"

Eliza raced back to the Commvee and told the ranger to check the Cleopatra's dock.

Sure enough, a small pile of walnut shells was right on the dock. And everyone saw the bright green parrot feather on top of the shells.

"Ahem!" The ranger huffed. "All right, you may go."

Eliza was excited. "Come on," she shouted to her family. "The Léons have a head start, but we're still in the race!"

Chapter 4

Nigel used the Commvee's top speed to catch up with the Cleopatra. Even so, when they reached their first stop, San Cristóbal Island, it was already night. Visitors weren't allowed into wild areas after dark, so the Thornberrys had to wait until the next day to look for animals.

In the morning, Eliza could hardly wait to explore. She looked towards Cerro

Brujo, a hill formed by the crumbling cone of an old volcano.

"You know, Deb," she said to her sister, "some of the tortoises here are over a hundred years old. Maybe they met Darwin."

"Do I look like I care?" Debbie asked, wiggling her toes. "Hey, Donnie, what do you think?"

"Urrrggggg," Donnie grinned. He had painted stripes on his belly with Debbie's nail polish. Then he aimed the brush at Darwin's nose.

"Ah-hoo-hoo-hoo!" Darwin yelled, running around the roof with his arms in the air.

"What's the hubbub?" asked Nigel, popping up to the roof. "No time for that, pets, we must go ashore!"

Debbie pointed to her freshly painted toenails. "I've got to stay here to let these babies dry. Don't worry, I'll keep Donnie by me."

Eliza grabbed a red notebook from her desk. "I wrote down all the things we have to find in this notebook," she told Darwin. "Charles Darwin carried one just like it."

That afternoon, just as Debbie was painting her fingernails for the fifth time, Damien Léon appeared.

"I can't believe my luck finding you alone!" he said to Debbie. "Want to go to Kicker Rock? It's not far and we might see blue-footed boobies."

Debbie didn't care about birds, but she didn't want Damien to know that. "Uh, sure," she said. "C'mon, Donnie."

Damien frowned. "*No* baby-sitting," he said.

Debbie wouldn't leave Donnie behind. So Damien finally agreed to let Donnie come. But as soon as they were out in the bay, Damien tipped the boat into a wave.

Donnie went flying and landed in the water!

"Wait! Go back!" Debbie screamed.

Damien just sped up. "Forget it. The little runt's probably home by now," he said. "If we go back for him, we'll never reach Kicker Rock before sunset."

Debbie argued, but Damien kept steering out to sea. In the meantime, Donnie had swum back to the Commvee. He howled and shook his dripping fists at the boat as it roared out of sight.

Hours later, Eliza was heading back to the Commvee with Darwin and her parents. They'd found many animals on the small island after a hard climb to the highlands above the bay.

Eliza lagged behind to chat with a giant tortoise. Suddenly she heard her mother call out, "Eliiiiiizaaaa!" Eliza ran back to the Commvee to find her parents pacing in the sand. "Your sister's missing!"

Chapter 5

"Daaaalabaruck. NOgodoneee."

Nigel and Marianne were trying to figure out what Donnie was saying – and keep away from his feet. He kept trying to kick them.

Just then they saw the Léons set sail for the next stop.

Eliza was mad. "Now we'll never win!"

"Eliza! The race isn't important right now," Marianne said. "We have to find Debbie!"

"I know," Eliza said. "It's just not fair, that's all."

Nigel and Marianne went to get flashlights. As Eliza watched the sun begin to sink, she thought about Debbie being alone somewhere. All of a sudden the race didn't seem all that important to Eliza either.

"Let me help look!" she cried.

Nigel placed his hand on her shoulder. "Now, poppet, we don't want both of you getting lost. Wait right here and let us know by radio when she gets back."

He and Marianne hurried off along the beach. Eliza waited exactly one minute. "We have to do something!" she told Darwin.

"KICKeriibbiiii!" Donnie howled. He aimed a kick at Darwin that made the chimp run around in circles.

Eliza suddenly understood. "Debbie's at Kicker Rock!"

She grabbed her flashlight. "Come on,

Darwin!" Eliza called as she started tugging the Thornberrys' motorboat towards the water.

"Don't you think we should wait for your parents? Someone's got to stay on the radio —"

"No time — it's getting dark," Eliza said, starting up the motor. Moaning, Darwin climbed in too. Donnie jumped in right after him.

Soon they were buzzing by the two stony pieces that made up Kicker Rock. A big wave tossed their boat up and down. "I knew this was a bad idea!" Darwin yelled.

"Relax, Darwin, I know what I'm doing," Eliza said. But the truth was Eliza was scared, too. The rising tide was pulling the boat closer to the jagged edges of Kicker Rock. And it was getting too dark to see.

Suddenly she heard a shout. "Eliza! Over here!"

It was Debbie! Eliza steered the boat towards her sister, who was clinging to a ledge, trying to keep above the waves.

"Daaalabruck!" Donnie shouted.

"Are you okay?" Eliza called out.

"OKAY? Are you crazy?" Debbie spit out salt water and swam towards the boat. "Look at my hair!"

Darwin helped Eliza pull her water-logged sister over the side of the boat.

"What happened?" Eliza asked.

"Thanks to that toad, Damien, I almost drowned!" Debbie spluttered. "He told me to climb onto a ledge to get some dumb boobie feather. Then he took off! The tide came up so I got stuck here."

When the girls got back, Nigel and Marianne were frantic.

"Heavens," Nigel said, mopping his brow when he heard their story. "What a narrow escape!" Eliza could tell he was upset at the idea that his idol might stoop to sabotage.

"I'm sure it was just a misunderstanding," Nigel said. "Leo Léon would never do such a thing."

Marianne didn't agree. "*You* wouldn't, Nigel, but Leo isn't as great as you think."

"He's tip-top in his field," Nigel argued, "the absolute *crème de la crème*."

"He's no *crème*, Nigel, he's a crumb," Marianne said. "You're more tip-top than he is, and it's time you realised it."

"Mum's right," Eliza chimed in.

Nigel blushed the colour of a red-hot chili pepper. Then he proudly twirled his moustache. "Well, er, if that's what you think . . . there's only one thing to do."

"What's that, Dad?" Debbie asked.

"Prove the Thornberrys are better, pumpkin . . . win this race!"

Chapter 6

Nigel steered the Commvee full steam ahead to Floreana Island. At sunrise, they started on their checklist. Their trail began on a beach covered in green sand.

"This is some wacky sand," Debbie said, scooping up a handful. "Maybe I'll paint my toenails this colour next time."

"Forget about your toes for a minute, Debbie," Eliza said, holding up a picture of a small drab-looking bird, "and help us look for this finch."

Debbie shrugged. "Why don't we just take its picture on some other island? Damien said finches are all over the Galápagos."

"The medium tree finch lives only on Floreana Island, pet," Nigel explained. He started telling her all about the thirteen different kinds of finches Darwin had found, but Debbie's eyes quickly glazed over.

"Just remember," Eliza said, "if we don't find a medium tree finch here, we don't win."

They headed off into the hills near a lagoon, collecting shots of some flamingos and other birds along the way. Eliza shivered as she looked at the twisted, dead-looking branches of the palo santo trees nearby. They reminded her of the creepy tales she had read about mysterious disappearances on this lonely island.

By the end of the day, the Thornberrys had spotted every animal on their list for the island, except the finch. It seemed to have disappeared as well.

While the Thornberrys took a break at the dock, the Léons returned. Eliza half wished they would vanish off Floreana Island, too, as the family piled aboard the Cleopatra and set off for the next stop.

"I guess that means they found the finch," Marianne sighed. "It's getting late. If we don't see one soon, we'll be here another day."

"Oh, I know what will cheer everyone up," Nigel said. He stepped into the Commvee and came out carrying a big plate.

"Uh-oh," Eliza groaned.

"Look, everyone! Kippers!" Nigel called out, smiling happily.

The second the plate hit the picnic table, Donnie moved in.

"Now, lad, leave a few for us," Nigel said. "I'm sure we'd all like some."

Donnie started flinging the fish around.

"Look out!" Eliza yelled.

"Incoming!" Debbie hollered. They both ducked under the table.

The next kipper hit Darwin – *SMACK!* – on the nose. He howled. "Ah-oo-ee-ee!"

Darwin ran around with his hands over his face, right into a tree! "Yowwww!"

The chimpanzee whimpered as he lay on the ground. Some leaves and a little brown blob dropped out of the tree and onto his belly.

"Are you okay?" Eliza ran over.

"No, I most certainly am not! That kipper smarted. And it stinks!" Darwin whined.

"I didn't mean you, Darwin," Eliza said. She gently picked up the small blob. The

blob ruffled its feathers and two bright eyes emerged.

"Say, how'd you know my name is Darwin?" the bird asked.

Eliza grinned. They were following the path of Charles Darwin with a chimp named Darwin. Now this bird had the same name, too?

"Your name is Darwin?" she asked the bird.

"All us finches here are named after Darwin, who noticed our very beautiful beaks," the bird said, showing off its own.

"Hey, you're a medium tree finch, aren't you?" Eliza asked. "Would you mind if we took your picture?"

As it turned out, there was nothing the bird would have liked more.

Soon Marianne was filming the finch as it sat on a branch. "Why, it's almost as if he's posing," she marvelled.

Chapter 7

With every species on Floreana Island accounted for, the Thornberrys set off for Isabela Island. There, the easiest animals to spot were the sea iguanas Charles Darwin had called "alligators in miniature." They swam right by the Commvee.

It was hot and dusty. When the Thornberrys found all the animals on the island, they returned to the Commvee.

Eliza spotted the Léons' parrot staggering around their vehicle.

"What's that mangy bird doing here?" Darwin asked Eliza.

"Dizzy!" Eliza heard the bird mutter. "Oooh . . . my aching head."

Eliza noticed that Napoleon's beak was covered with scratches. But before she could help him, the parrot took off. He zigzagged towards the Cleopatra, which set sail soon after he landed.

Marianne and Eliza shrugged their shoulders. Debbie climbed into the Commvee for a drink. A second later she was back.

"Hey, what's up with the water?" asked Debbie.

"Why? What's wrong with it?" Marianne asked in reply.

"Nothing, that's what," Debbie said. She held up an empty glass. Everyone piled inside. They tried every sink and shower in the Commvee. No water anywhere.

Then they went outside to check the tanks. They all gasped. The tanks were pitted with holes!

"How could this happen?" Marianne asked.

"It's the Léons!" Eliza said. "Edmond must've made his bird poke holes in the tanks!"

"Now, Eliza," Nigel said. "You can't just go around accusing people without proof."

He simply could not imagine Leo Léon trying to win the race by trickery. Then Eliza spotted bird tracks and what looked to be a boy's footprints in the wet sand below the tanks.

Nigel sighed and shook his head. He finally accepted that his idol Leo would do anything to win. "Well," Nigel said. "I

certainly won't trust that chap again."

"About time," Debbie muttered.

"Don't be rude to your father," Marianne snapped. "Even if he should have known Leo was a louse."

"Marianne!" Nigel huffed.

Pretty soon they all were arguing. Even Donnie seemed upset. He was running around in circles and hooting. "FooooOG Hadadada. FooooOG."

"Now look what you've done!" Nigel scolded. "That may look like the Tibetan fog-calling dance but I'm sure it's just the lad's way of showing he's upset."

Worse yet, the race rules said they had to return to Santa Cruz for more water. By the time they reached the research station, no one was talking to anyone else, except for Eliza and Darwin.

"We'll never win now," Eliza said to Darwin. The two of them were walking through the station while the tanks were being fixed. "Not with everyone fighting. And not if those sneaky Léons keep cheating."

They walked by a huge tortoise sitting in the sun. Eliza read the sign in front of its pen.

"This is so sad, Darwin," she said. "He's called Lonesome George because he's the last of his kind."

"What do you mean? We've seen lots of giant turtles," Darwin said.

"There are all different kinds. George is the very last one just like him."

"It's terrible being the only one of your kind," said the tortoise. He had moved slowly closer to Eliza and Darwin.

Eliza introduced herself and Darwin. "We're here with my family."

"Family." George sighed. "What a wonderful word."

"I guess," sighed Eliza. "Although sometimes it isn't always easy being in one."

"You never know what it means to be part of a family until you don't have one anymore," George said sadly. "I might not be in this mess if my family had just learnt to adapt. We liked living spread out all over our island. If we had stuck together instead, we might have been able to save the family."

Eliza nodded. "George, you're absolutely right. And there's something I've got to do – right now!"

Chapter 8

"We all have to get along!"

Marianne looked up from the water tank when Eliza came running up.

"Eliza, honey, I'm glad you're back. I'm sorry I acted so grumpy before."

Nigel popped his head out of a window. "Likewise, luvs. I think we were in a bit of a kerfluffle. But all's cheery now, arr-arr!" He came out to give them all a big hug.

Eliza said. "If we're ever going to beat

the Léons, we're going to have to stick together – as a family."

"Well, duh!" said Debbie. "But we don't stand a chance unless something happens to the Léons. Like getting lost at sea."

"How about a little fog instead?" Nigel asked with a toothy grin.

He explained that he had just heard the weather report. The famous Galápagos fog was rolling in – the worst anyone had seen in years.

"Fog? Like the kind you get when you do a Tibetan fog-calling dance?" Eliza asked. Everyone turned to stare at Donnie, who had his toes in his mouth.

"Well, their ship looks like it can find its way through anything," Debbie grumbled.

"Don't fret, poodles," said Nigel. "A beastly fog can work wonders on high-tech motors, too." He looked at them. "What do you say we give it a go, eh?"

Marianne raced for the driver's seat. Debbie closed all the hatches. Eliza and Darwin sat by the radio, listening for more weather reports.

Nigel muttered something about "that kipper thingee" and disappeared below with a wrench.

The Commvee raced on. They didn't see the fog until it surrounded them like a giant cloud. Soon everything on board was dripping.

Suddenly Eliza yelled, "Guess what I just heard on the radio? The Léons have lost power! They haven't even made it to Santiago Island yet!"

"Hooray!" Marianne, Debbie, and Eliza shouted.

The Commvee's motor purred on for a while. When their locator became too wet to work, Marianne's expert map-reading led them right to Santiago.

The Thornberrys landed on the island at dawn. They climbed out of the Commvee just as the Cleopatra sailed in.

"Quick, pets," Nigel shouted. "We haven't got much of a head start!"

They all took off. Everyone kept an eye out for the animals and plants on Eliza's list.

By midday the list was done. "And it's all thanks to *moi*," said Debbie.

Debbie had spotted the rare land iguana, almost stepping on its tail when she wandered off the trail.

Marianne got a good shot of the shy yellow lizard before it ran away. She also got a good shot of Debbie yelling as she ran the *other* way.

Now it was time to head back to Santa Cruz. The rangers would be waiting to see who arrived first.

"Look, there's the Cleopatra!" Eliza

pointed to the bay. It was just chugging out to sea.

Everyone raced to the Commvee. Soon they were catching up to the Cleopatra, which was moving very slowly. Their ship's motor groaned. There was too much fog water in the fuel.

"They'll never make it!" Eliza shouted.

Just then the Commvee gave a low groan too. And a second later, the motor stopped.

"Looks like *we're* not going to make it, either," said Debbie.

Chapter 9

BRROOM! Brroom! The Commvee started up again with a roar even louder than before. Eliza gasped.

Nigel climbed up from the engineering area. He had a greasy smear on his nose.

"Dad! What did you do?" Eliza asked, giving him a big hug.

Nigel twirled the wrench on one finger. "I told you I was going to give the motor a bit of a fix, what? I hooked it up to a new source of power: waterproof gasoline made of kipper oil!"

"I used up my whole supply," Nigel added sadly. "But there's enough to get to Santa Cruz Island."

The Commvee charged ahead. Soon it was neck and neck with the Cleopatra. Eliza could see Leo glaring at them.

The two ships were almost at the dock, which was crowded with people. Rangers waited with stopwatches.

"We're winning!" Eliza shouted, at the same moment that the Commvee ran out of kipper oil. The Thornberrys stared at each other in dismay as the Commvee drifted to a stop.

"Paddle!" Eliza yelled.

They all climbed down to the Commvee's big floats. Everyone started paddling. But the Cleopatra was gaining. And just as they reached the dock, the Cleopatra pulled ahead.

"Lost by a whisker!" Nigel gasped.

"It isn't over yet!" cried Eliza. She ran inside to get her notebook and Marianne's film. Then they went down to the dock.

"*Voila!* Behold the winner: Leo Léon, King of the Beasts!" Leo was shouting to the crowd. Then he waved at everyone as though he were really some kind of king.

But the ranger held up his hand. "The winner won't be announced until we have checked off all the animals on the lists!" he said.

The rangers went into the station while the Thornberrys and Léons waited outside. Leo started signing autographs – and charging for them.

Eliza and Darwin went to visit Lonesome George. He seemed a lot happier. The rangers had introduced him to a female tortoise from another family.

Finally the ranger came back out. "We checked the lists. We watched the films," the ranger announced. "And the winner is . . ."

Leo Léon began to bow.

"The Thornberrys!"

The crowd cheered.

"WHAT?" Leo roared.

It turned out the Léons had spotted only twelve different kinds of finches. Darwin had counted thirteen.

"You forgot the medium tree finch," the ranger said. "The Thornberrys didn't." He gave Eliza a wink before walking off.

Leo was practically purple with rage. He stormed away with his family, and the Cleopatra took off in a puff of sour black smoke.

"I guess they should have looked up Darwin's finches like you did, squirt," Debbie said, tugging one of Eliza's pigtails.

"If the Léons had spent less time

playing tricks and more time learning what they needed to stay in the race, they would have won," Marianne said.

"No, they wouldn't," said Debbie. She and Marianne burst out laughing. Nigel started to "arr-arr" along with them. Darwin and Donnie joined in.

Eliza got the giggles too. "This is the 'survival of the Thornberrys!'"

Discovery Facts

Blue-footed booby: A bird with sky-blue webbed feet found on many of the Galápagos Islands.

Darwin: Sir Charles Darwin: A naturalist who visited the Galápagos Islands in 1835.

Ecuador: A country in South America.

Finch: A type of bird. Darwin observed thirteen different kinds of finches in the Galápagos.

Floreana Island (also called Santa María): An island in the Galápagos that was named Charles when Darwin visited.

Galápagos Islands: An "archipelago," or group of islands, 600 miles west of Ecuador.

Iguana: A type of large lizard. The sea, or marine, iguana of the Galápagos is the only sea-going lizard in the world. The land iguana is bright yellow.

Isabela Island: The biggest island in the Galápagos; known as Albermarle when Darwin visited.

Kicker Rock: A large rock off the coast of San Cristóbal Island, it's all that remains of the cone of an old volcano.

Lonesome George: A real-life tortoise who lives at the Charles Darwin Research Station. He is the last of the Pinta Island tortoises.

Penguins: Large flightless sea birds. Penguins can live in the Galápagos because of a cold current that passes nearby.

San Cristóbal Island: One of the Galápagos islands; named Chatham at the time of Darwin's visit.

Santa Cruz Island: The site of the Charles Darwin Research Station and the most populated island in the Galápagos.

Santiago Island (also called San Salvador): An island in the Galápagos; it was called James when Darwin visited.

Survival of the Fittest: The theory that only the strongest members of a species will survive and reproduce. Over time, the whole species grows stronger as those traits are passed along.

Tortoise: A turtle-like reptile that can weigh as much as 550 pounds, and live 150 years or longer. Once fourteen kinds of tortoises lived in the Galápagos, now there are just eleven.

Darwin
and the Galápagos

In 1831, Charles Darwin set sail from England on the *Beagle*. He was going on a four-year journey around the coasts of South America.

The young scientist was fascinated with the idea of "natural selection," the belief that species of animals and plants can change over time – sometimes becoming a whole different species! Many people did not agree with this idea.

But Darwin's observations of plants and animals on the *Beagle's* visit to the Galápagos Islands helped to change that. He wrote about his findings in the 1859 book, *Origin of Species*. It caused an uproar! For the first time, someone offered proof that the theory of natural selection could be true.

Today scientists still debate Darwin's ideas. And the islands are protected so that modern visitors can have a firsthand look at Darwin's observations.

About the Author

Maria Rosado has written more than a dozen books for young readers, using a number of pen names, as well as stories for *Nickelodeon Magazine* and other publications for children.

She shares a tiny apartment in New York City with her cartoon-loving husband, one cat, and hundreds of books. Maria grew up in New Jersey and when she was younger, she kept a little turtle as a pet – but it escaped. Maria thinks it could have swum off to the Galápagos Islands to commune with the tortoises!